Mm

Gg Hh Ii Jj Kk Ll

Uu Vv Ww Xx Yy Zz

Dear Parent,

The My First Steps to Reading® *series is based on a teaching activity that helps children learn to recognize letters and their sounds. The use of predictable language patterns and repetition of familiar words will also help your child build a basic sight vocabulary. Your child will enjoy watching the characters in the books place imaginative objects in "letter boxes." You and your child can even create and fill your own letter box, using stuffed animals, cut-out pictures, or other objects beginning with the same letter. The things you can do together are limited only by your imagination. Learning letters will be fun—the first important step on the road to reading.*

The Editors

My "w" Book

(The "wh" sound is included in this book.)

written by Jane Belk Moncure
illustrated by Colin King

Little  had a box.

"I will find things that begin
with my 'w' sound," she said.

"I will put them into my sound box."

Little  went for a walk in the woods. She found . . .

woodpeckers

and a woodchuck.

Did she put them into her box? She did.

Little  looked under some wood chips. She found lots of wiggly worms.

"In you go," she said.

Little  walked to a well in the woods. She drank some water from the well.

"This may be a wishing well," she said. She looked all around the well.

Guess what she found? It was a wand.

Little  waved her wand and made a wish.

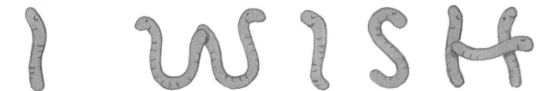

"I wish I could find more things for my box," she said.

Just then,

a weasel  wiggled into the box
as quick as a wink.

A big wolf was after him!

Little  waved her wand.

"I wish you would
be a good wolf,"
she said.
She put the wolf
into her box with

the weasel, the woodpecker,
the wiggly worms, and the woodchuck.

Now the box was full.

Little  found a wheelbarrow.

"Wow," she said.
"This is just what I need."
Away they went . . .

up and down a winding road to the water.

"Let's wade in the water," she said.

But the wolf, weasel, woodpecker, wiggly worms, and woodchuck did not want to wade. They watched.

"Wow," said a walrus.

"You look wacky to me.
You have funny feet."

"You look wacky to me," said Little .

"You have funny whiskers," she said.

Little  put the walrus into the box.

The walrus winked at the wolf.

Little  went back to the water.

The wind blew the waves up and down.

Then she saw . . .

a big whale in the water.

"I wish I could put the whale in my box,
but the whale is too big," she said.

Little  waved her wand and found a big wooden cart.

It was big enough for everything!

She put all of her things into it
and walked into . . .

a wall.

What was behind the wall?

"Whoopee," whooped the woodpecker when he saw the

watermelons.

"Let's have a watermelon party,"

said Little . And they did.

wolf

wheelbarrow

watermelons

wiggly worms

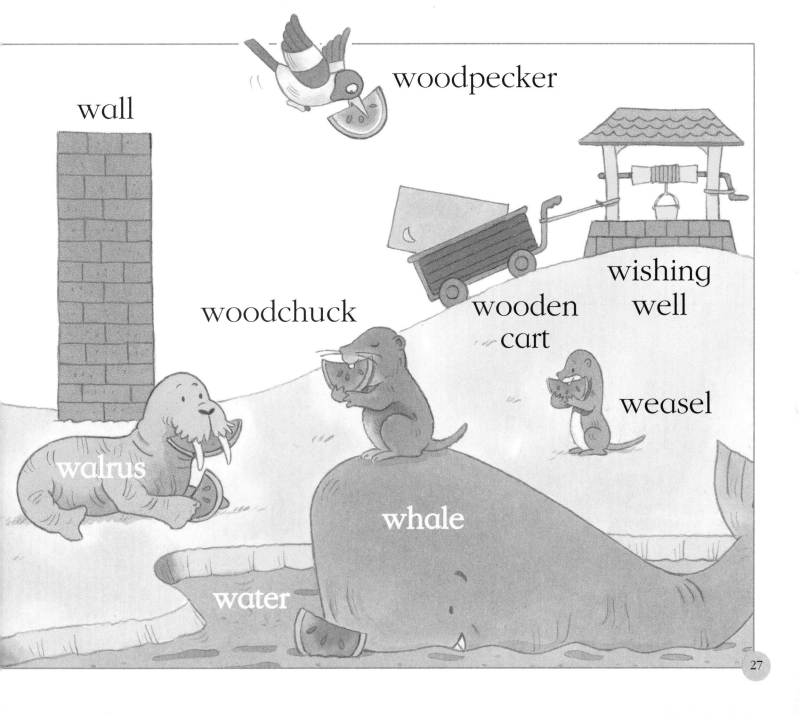

woodpecker

wall

wishing
well

woodchuck

wooden
cart

weasel

walrus

whale

water

Can you read these words

with Little  ?

watch

window

woman

wallet

web

28

waffle

wig

windmill

whistle

willow

wheel

Aa Bb Cc Dd Ee Ff

Nn Oo Pp Qq Rr Ss Tt

My First
Steps to
READING®